TESS OF THE D'URBERVILLES

TESS OF THE D'URBERVILLES

Thomas Hardy

Om KIDZ
An imprint of Om Books International

First published in 2019 by

Om Kidz | Om Books International

Corporate & Editorial Office
A-12, Sector 64, Noida 201 301
Uttar Pradesh, India
Phone: +91 120 477 4100
Email: editorial@ombooks.com
Website: www.ombooksinternational.com

Sales Office
107, Ansari Road, Darya Ganj
New Delhi 110 002, India
Phone: +91 11 4000 9000
Email: sales@ombooks.com
Website: www.ombooks.com

Retold by Swayam Ganguly

ISBN: 978-93-85031-57-1

Printed in India

10 9 8 7 6 5 4 3 2 1

Contents

Chapter One

Sir John

On a late May evening, a middle-aged man was walking home to the village of Marlott, in the adjoining vale of Blackmoor. He walked on rickety legs and a fault in his gait made him incline a bit to the left of a straight line. An empty egg-basket rested on his arm and he was wearing an old hat. He was soon met by an elderly parson riding a grey mare. "Good night," the man said.

"Good night, Sir John," the Parson replied.

"Beg your pardon, sir," the man said, turning around. "You addressed me as 'Sir John' last market-day, and once before a month ago. Why did you do so when I am plain Jack Durbeyfield, the haggler?"

The parson said after a moment's hesitation, "It was because of a discovery I made, hunting for pedigrees for the history of the new county. I'm Parson Tringham, the antiquary of Stagfoot Lane. But Durbeyfield, aren't you aware that you are the lineal representative of the old knightly family of the d'Urbervilles, who are descended from Sir Pagan d'Urberville, the famous knight who arrived from Normandy with William the Conqueror, from Battle Abbey Roll?"

"I've never heard that before, sir."

"Well, it's the truth. Throw up your chin now, so I can see the profile better. Yes, that's the chin and nose of a d'Urberville all right, a little debased though! Let me tell you that your ancestor was one of the twelve knights in Normandy, who aided the Lord of Estremavilla to conquer Glamorganshire. Branches of your family held manors in this part of England, with their names appearing in the pipe rolls at the reign of King Stephen. One of them was so rich at the time of King John's reign that he gifted a manor to the Knights Hospitallers. Your forefather Brian, was summoned to attend the Great Council at Westminster

during Edward the Second's reign and you did decline a bit during Oliver Cromwell's time. On account of your loyalty, you were made Knights of the Royal Oak, during the rule of Charles the Second. There have been generations of Sir Johns in your family, and if knighthood was hereditary like a baronetcy, like in the olden times where men were knighted from father to son, you would be Sir John now."

"Ye don't say that!"

"In short, there's hardly such a family in England," the Parson concluded.

"Daze my eyes! How long hev you knowed this news about me Parson Tringham?"

The clergyman explained that this news was so old that it had died out. He had learned about this during his own investigations when he was engaged to trace out the lineage of the d'Urberville family.

"Well, I heard a couple of times that my family had seen better days before coming to Blackmoor, but didn't think too much of it. But Parson, where do we d'Urbervilles live now?"

"Nowhere. As a country family, you are extinct. Gone under."

"Where do we lie?"

"Plenty of you can be found in rows and rows, in your vaults at Kingsbere-sub-Greenhill."

"What about our family mansions and estates?"

"You haven't any. No lands either, although you had plenty once."

"Shall we ever regain our former glory?"

"Ah, I can't tell," the clergyman replied.

"What do I do about it, sir?" Durbeyfield enquired.

"Oh, nothing except maybe think about how low you have fallen. In fact, several families that live in the cottages of this county can boast of such an illustrious lineage. Goodnight!"

After the clergyman left, a stunned Durbeyfield sat down on the grassy bank by the road. After a few minutes, a youth appeared. But the boy reacted strongly when Durbeyfield ordered him to go on an errand for him. "Who do you think you are John Durbeyfield, to order me about?"

"That's the secret, Fred. Now, take the message because the secret is that I belong to a noble race. I have just discovered that I am Sir John d'Urberville, and it is recorded in history about me. Do you know of a place called Kingsbere-sub-Greenhill?"

"Aye, I have been to Greenhill Fair."

"Hundreds of my ancestors lie there under the church of that parish. They rest in coats of mail and jewels in great, heavy lead coffins. No man in South-Wessex has a nobler family than me."

"Oh?"

"Now carry my basket and go to The Pure Drop Inn. Ask them to send me a horse and a carriage immediately to carry me home. They should put a small bottle of rum at the bottom of the carriage and charge it to my account. Then, go to my house with the basket; and tell my wife to stop washing, and wait for me till I reach home as I have news to tell her."

The boy still looked in two minds. So, Durbeyfield handed him a shilling. "That's for your labour, lad!"

"Thank you, Sir John! Is there anything else I can do for you, Sir John?"

"Tell them at home that I would like lamb's fry for supper. If they fail to get it, black-pot and if they can't get that too, chitterlings will do."

"Yes, Sir John."

The lad left, and Durbeyfield waited as evening set in slowly.

Chapter Two

Tess Durbeyfield

The village of Marlott was located amidst the beautiful Vale of Blakemore, or Blackmoor. The vale was a fertile and sheltered area where the springs were never dry and the fields, never brown. In former times, the Vale was known as the Forest of White Hart, a name derived from a curious legend. During King Henry III's reign, he had prevented a certain Thomas de la Lynd from killing a beautiful white hart, penalizing the offender heavily. The forests of yesteryears might have disappeared but the old customs like the May-Day dance still remained. This was to be viewed that afternoon, although it was more dancing than walking and mostly, by the younger members of the fairer sex.

This party of merry country girls arrived at The Pure Drop Inn. "The Load-a-Lord!" one of them exclaimed. "Look, Tess Durbeyfield! Your father is riding home in a carriage!"

A young member of the group turned her head. She was a handsome girl with innocent eyes and a red ribbon in her hair. She saw Durbeyfield moving in a chaise, driven by a brawny woman who was the servant of the Pure Drop. Durbeyfield was leaning back, eyes closed and singing slowly- "I've got a great family vault at Kingsbere and knighted forefathers in lead coffins too!"

Everyone in the club tittered, except Tess, who was angry that her father was making a fool of himself in public. "He's just tired," she said quickly. "He got a lift home as our own horse is resting today."

"Bless you for being so simple, Tess," her companions laughed. "He's got his market-nitch. Ha ha!"

"I shan't walk an inch with you if you crack any jokes about him," Tess warned them, as she turned red. Instantly, her eyes grew moist, and she looked downwards. Her companions didn't say another word for fear that they

had hurt her and soon Tess was merry again when they reached the dancing enclosure.

Tess was a country girl who was all emotion and little experience. Her childhood had still not abandoned her completely and one could discern her ninth year sparkling from her eyes sometimes or her twelfth year on her cheeks. Strangers would stare at her, fascinated. But in reality, Tess was just a superb specimen of a country girl and nothing more!

Durbeyfield was soon forgotten as the girls entered the enclosure and the dancing began. The girls danced with each other as there were no males. But soon, as the hour for labour to close was approaching, the men began to gather around the enclosure. In this crowd, were three young men belonging to a superior class. They held stout sticks and carried small knapsacks strapped to their shoulders. It was clear that they were brothers. The first was dressed as a curate, the second as an undergraduate and the third was dressed in a casual manner that suggested he was unemployed.

It was learnt that the three brothers were holidaying by a walking tour through the Vale of Blackmoor from the town of Shaston. The two elder brothers were in a hurry and not inclined to dance but the youngest wanted to.

"All right, Felix," the younger one declared. "I'll catch up with you and Cuthbert in five minutes. Carry on and don't stop for me."

The elder brothers left reluctantly, carrying their younger brother's knapsack who entered the field through the gate.

"It's a thousand pities that you dance alone," he stated gallantly to the girls near him. "Where are your partners, my dears?"

"They're still at work," the boldest one replied. "They'll be here soon. Till then, will you be one, sir?"

"Certainly. But what's one among so many?"

"Better than none. Now pick and choose."

The young man chose the girl nearest him as he could not pick and choose so quickly among so many girls. It was not the girl he had spoken to as she had expected, nor was it Tess. The chosen girl was envied by

all the others for having danced with such a handsome man. The young man had set such a powerful force of example that soon, the other village men entered by the gate and had chosen their partners.

The church hour struck and the young man declared that he would have to leave. As he left the dance, his eyes fell suddenly on Tess. He observed the reproach in her eyes that he had not chosen her and felt a sense of regret that he hadn't noticed her before. Then, he started running because of his lengthy delay. Reaching a high rise, he stopped to catch his breath, and looked back. He saw the white figures of the girls dancing as he had left them. They seemed to have forgotten him already. Except one! She stood by the hedge alone, staring at his receding back. It was the same girl who had been hurt at not being chosen and whom, he wished he had chosen. It was a trifle matter, but at least, he should have asked her name. She was so modest and yet so expressive. Dismissing the matter from his head, he turned and walked away rapidly.

Chapter Three

Domestic Problems

Tess could not bring herself to dance for a long time after the young man had left! Many partners presented themselves, but alas, none of them spoke as nicely as the stranger. It was only when the stranger's figure had completely receded in the horizon did Tess consent to dance with a partner. Tess retreated homewards at sunset, while she thought of her poor father. Her heart was anyway, no longer in the dance.

As she came closer home, familiar sounds greeted her. A cradle was being violently rocked on a stone floor to the tune of a song by a loud, feminine voice. Tess opened the door to face the one-candled dreary, yellow spectacle. Her mother stood over the Monday washing-tub just as

Tess had left her, surrounded by her children. Tess felt the usual regret that she should have helped her mother in the domestic chores instead of stepping outdoors.

Mrs. Durbeyfield stood on one foot doing the washing while she rocked the cradle of her youngest child with the other foot. The cradle in its last stage, creaked its tune just like Joan Durbeyfield, despite being burdened.

"Let me help you rock the cradle or with the washing, mother," Tess offered.

Tess's mother had no ill-feeling towards her daughter for having gone outdoors while she had had to do the household work. Her plan to do the work all by herself was simply to postpone them.

"Well, I'm glad you have arrived, Tess. I can go and fetch your father now. But more than that, I want to tell you what has happened."

"Has it got something to do with father doing silly things in that carriage?" Tess enquired. "I almost sank to the ground in shame."

"Well, your father discovered that we were the greatest gentlefolk in the country, dating right back to the times

of the Pagan Turks. Monuments, vaults, crests and Lord knows what all are in our name. We were made Knights o' the Royal Oak in Saint Charles's days, and our real name was d'Urberville. That was why your father rode home and not because he had been drinking, as people thought."

"I'm glad to hear that, mother. But will that do us any good?"

"Oh yes. Many great things might come out of it. Many people of our rank might ride down here in carriages as soon as the news is known. Your father learnt the news in Shaston and..."

"Where is father?" Tess interrupted.

"He visited the doctor in Shaston today. It seems that consumption is not the problem. It is fat around the heart. The doctor said your father might last ten years, ten months, or ten days."

"But where is father now?" an alarmed Tess asked again.

"The poor man went to Rolliver's half an hour ago to relieve himself at the parson's news. He wants to gather his strength for the journey tomorrow to deliver that

load of beehives. He will have to start a little after twelve tonight, the journey being so long."

"Go to a public-house to regain his strength?" Tess asked incredulously. "How could you agree to it, mother?"

""No, I did not agree," her mother said defensively at the rebuke. "I've been waiting for you to come and keep house while I go and fetch him."

Tess offered to go, but her mother insisted that she would go. Tess knew what this meant. This was the only time when Mrs. Durbeyfield enjoyed while she pretended to go and look for her husband at the inn, in the muck and muddle of housework and rearing children. She would discover him at the inn and spend a couple of hours with him there, dismissing all thought of the children. This short respite made them both happy.

After her mother left, Tess got busy by sprinkling the linen dried during the day, in the company of her nine-year old brother Abraham and her twelve-year old sister Eliza-Louisa, called 'Liza-Lu', after the youngest ones had been put to bed. There was a gap of more than four years between Tess and her next sibling, and so she

assumed a semi- maternal role when she took care of the others. After Abraham, there were two more girls called Hope and Modesty; then a boy of three, and the baby who had just finished his first year. These were the six helpless passengers in the Durbeyfield ship, totally dependent on the adult Durbeyfields for everything under the sun.

Her parents didn't appear after a long time and a worried Tess looked outside to see the village shutting down. Candles and lamps were being extinguished and Tess was angry that a man who was to embark on a journey at one in the morning was at the inn so late celebrating his ancient legacy. Reluctantly, Tess asked Abraham not to be afraid and fetch his parents. Half an hour elapsed, but neither man, woman nor child returned. "I must go myself," Tess resolved. She put Liza-Lu to bed and locked all the children in. Then Tess made her way in the darkness to Rolliver's Inn.

Chapter Four

The Death of a Prince

Rolliver's Inn was the only alehouse in the village. As it only had an off-licence, one couldn't legally, drink there. So, the customers had limited seating arrangement in the form of a small board. In a large bedroom upstairs, a dozen of the privileged customers drank with the landlady, Mrs. Rolliver. Mrs. Durbeyfield was welcomed as she entered here and discovered her husband there gloating about his glorious ancient family history. "Don't sing so loud," Mrs. Rolliver warned Sir John. "A member of the Government could be passing by and could confiscate my licence."

"You heard what happened to us, I suppose?" Joan Durbeyfield asked her.

"Yes. Do you think there's some money in it?"

"I've heard that there's a rich lady at Trantridge named d'Urberville. She must be our relation. I think I'll send Tess to claim kin," Joan replied.

"Come to think of, there is a lady by that name, although the parson didn't mention her," Sir John replied. "But undoubtedly, she's a junior branch of us."

None of them had noticed little Abraham who had entered the room and was waiting for a chance to ask them to return home. "I don't see why two branches of one family shouldn't visit each other," Mrs. Durbeyfield declared.

"Yes, we'll all claim kin," Abraham exclaimed from under the bedstead. "We'll go and visit her when Tess goes to live with her and wear black clothes and ride in her coach."

"How did you come here, child? What nonsense are you speaking? Go and play outside till father and mother are ready. Well, Tess should go to this lady and she would surely win over her and some noble gentleman would surely marry her."

Although this conversation was meant to be private, it had been overheard by everyone in the room. But soon, they were silent as the subject of the conversation entered the room. The look of reproach in Tess's dark eyes was enough to make her parents rise from their seats hastily. The three went home, Tess and Mrs. Durbeyfield supporting Sir John with their hands, even though he had drunk very little. But the weakness in the man had caused him to be tipsy. "I've got a family vault at Kings-bere," he declared loudly, viewing the smallness of his present house as it came to sight.

"Hush, Jacky," his wife snapped.

"I'm afraid father won't be able to go with the beehives so early tomorrow morning!" Tess stated.

"I'll be all right in a few hours," Durbeyfield protested. The family went to bed at eleven and two o'clock was the time for the journey as the beehives were supposed to be delivered to the retailers before the Saturday market commenced. The distance was almost thirty miles and the horse and wagon were one of the slowest, if not the slowest.

"The poor man can't go," Tess's mother declared to her at one thirty in the morning. "But someone has to go," Tess protested. "As it is, it's late for the hives and swarming season will be over soon. We cannot afford to keep them for next week's market."

"But who will go?" her mother asked. "I shall go myself," Tess declared. "If Abraham keeps me company."

Tess's mother reluctantly agreed to this arrangement and little Abraham was woken up and dressed, while mentally still in the other world. The horse was reluctant as well to leave at this hour. But they were on their way soon. Abraham grew drowsy and Tess made him a nest with the hives as he slept, so he wouldn't fall off. As she rode, Tess reflected on her sad life, till she fell asleep herself. She awoke with a sudden jerk, realising that the wagon had stopped. Tess heard a terrible groan, unlike something she had never heard before. "Hoi there!" someone shouted from front. The lantern hanging in her wagon had been extinguished, and another one shone on her face. Something terrible had occurred as the harness was caught up with something that blocked the way.

Tess jumped down, and realised the bitter truth! The speeding morning mail-cart had crashed into her wagon, and its pointed shaft had entered poor Prince's body. Prince was bleeding from his wound and Tess tried to cover the gaping wound, and was covered in crimson. Tess stood helplessly as Prince died slowly! The mail-cart man arrived, but there was nothing he could do now! "You were on the wrong side," he stated to Tess, adding that he had to leave with the mail-bags but would send help soon. "Don't worry! It'll be daylight soon!"

After the man left, Tess waited, as the birds awoke and the sun rose. The blood from Prince's body spread further on the road, as the horse lay there with his eye half open. "It is all my doing," Tess wailed. "There's no excuse. What will father and mother live for now?" Tess woke up Abraham and they waited together in silence. The driver of the mail-cart sent a farmer's man, riding a strong cob. Tess's wagon was harnessed to it and the load was taken to Casterbridge. The same evening, the wagon returned to the same spot to hoist up whatever remained of Prince's dead body and journeyed

nine miles back to Marlott. Tess however, had gone home earlier to break the news. How she would break the news was foremost on her mind but thankfully her parents already knew of Prince's death. But no one else in the Durbeyfield family blamed Tess as much as she blamed herself. Durbeyfield rose to the occasion magnificently when it was discovered that the tanner and knacker were offering only a few shillings for Prince's disintegrated carcass. "No!" he declared firmly, "I shall not sell his body. When we were knights, we never sold the dead bodies of our horses. Let them keep their shillings. Prince has served me well during his lifetime and I won't part from him now."

He toiled the next day to create a grave for Prince in the garden than he had for months to create a crop for his family. When the hole was made, Durbeyfield and his wife tied the dead body with a rope and dragged it towards the hole, their children following in a funeral procession. Abraham and Liza-Lu cried; Hope and Modesty expressed their grief in loud bellows and they

gathered around the hole when Prince's body finally tumbled into it. Their bread-winner had gone and there was nothing they could do about it. "Has he gone to heaven?" Abraham asked, sobbing. Durbeyfield began shoveling in the earth and the children cried, with the exception of Tess. Her face was dry and white and she considered herself the murderess of Prince.

Chapter Five

Alec d'Urberville

The haggling business had depended mainly on the horse and now misery and penury seemed unavoidable for the Durbeyfields. Durbeyfield, who was locally considered lazy, did produce the ability to work hard periodically. But times were hard, and he was unused to the demanding working hours of a regular day-labourer. Tess was wondering how to get her parents out of this predicament, which she had gotten them into in the first place, when her mother provided the solution.

"Tess, you must visit the rich Mrs. d'Urberville, living on the outskirts of the Chase. She must be our relation and you must approach her to claim kin. She should help us in our hour of trouble."

Tess was more deferential to this outrageous suggestion because Tess could not comprehend her mother's insistence that she should be part of a scheme that appeared particularly distasteful to her.

"It's better if I try to get some work," Tess murmured her disapproval. Tess's mother asked her husband to persuade Tess.

"I don't approve of my children going and asking for help from strange kin," Durbeyfield stated. "I am the head of the noblest branch of my family and I should set an example."

But her father's reason for not doing what her mother suggested was worse than Tess's own objections. She agreed to give in to her mother's demands.

Tess woke up early the next day and walked to the hill-town called Shaston. She boarded a van from there that dropped her to Trantridge, the parish where the mysterious Mrs. d'Urberville resided. After reaching Trantridge Cross, Tess ascended a hill on foot to travel towards the district known as the Chase, on the borders of which the lady lived. It was a simple country-house built for pleasure and residential purposes, with a small

BRITISH MUSEUM

fancy farm tended by a bailiff. Everything was new, bright and moneyed right from the acres of glass houses to the stables partially screened by Austrian pines and evergreen oaks. Tess stood in front of the house, rather alarmed at this sight. "Everything here is quite new," she exclaimed inartistically. "I thought we were an old family."

The Stoke d'Urbervilles, as they first chose to call themselves, owned this property. It was unusual for such a family to exist in such an old-fashioned part of the country. The deceased Mr. Simon Stoke had amassed his fortune as a merchant (some said, a money-lender) in the North, and had decided to settle in the county in the South. He decided to choose a name that would not identify him with his past as a smart trader and not be common either. He spent an hour in the British Museum, poring over ancient works involving ruined families before choosing the name d'Urberville. Thus, the name was annexed for himself and his ancestors from the pages of history.

However, poor Tess and her parents were in total ignorance of this act of piracy and imagination. A tall

young man emerged from the door of the tent in the lawn. He looked almost barbaric, with a swarthy complexion, full lips and a groomed black moustache with curled points. The gentleman was about twenty three or twenty four years old and had a powerful personality despite his barbaric features. He was quite unlike the dignified, old man Tess had expected to meet. "What can I do for you, my beauty?" he enquired.

"I came to see your mother, sir," Tess replied.

"I'm afraid that's not possible. You see, she is an invalid," Mr. Alec, the only son of the deceased Simon Stoke replied. "May I answer your purpose? What is your business?"

"I can't say its business, sir."

"Pleasure?"

"Oh no, sir! It's so foolish that I can't tell you," Tess confessed.

"I like foolish things. Try me, my dear," he said kindly.

"Mother asked me to come, and I wasn't too keen on coming myself. We are of the same family as you."

"Ho! Poor relations?"

"Yes, sir."

"Stokes?"

"No, sir. d'Urbervilles."

"Yes, yes, d'Urbervilles."

"Our names have worn away to Durbeyfield but we have sufficient evidence that we are d 'Urbervilles, like the old seal marked with a ramping lion on a shield, and a castle over him. We also have an old silver spoon, round in the bowl like a little ladle, marked with the same castle."

"A castle argent is definitely my crest, and my arms a rampant lion," he replied drily.

"My mother said we ought to make ourselves known to you, as we've lost our horse, owing to a bad accident and as we are the oldest branch in the family."

"That's very kind of your mother," he stated with a look that made Tess blush. "So, pretty girl, you've visited us as a relation then?"

"I suppose so," Tess replied uncomfortably.

"There's no harm in that," he said, and enquired where she lived. Tess gave him the details, stating that she intended to return by the same carrier that had fetched her. He invited Tess to take a walk in the grounds with him and gave her a tour of the lawns, flower-beds, conservatories, fruit-garden and greenhouses. He insisted

on feeding her a strawberry himself and filled her little basket with strawberries. He also prepared a small luncheon box for her without bothering the servants so this pleasant tete-a tete wouldn't be interrupted. Tess felt Alec d'Urberville's eyes riveted upon her and this troubled her. "I am going home now, sir," she declared, after finishing her light lunch.

"What do they call you?" he asked, as he walked her along the drive away from the house.

"Tess Durbeyfield, sir."

"You said your people have lost your horse?"

"I killed him," Tess declared, her eyes brimming with tears, as she narrated the full story.

"If I cannot do anything, I'm sure my mother should find a berth for you," he stated. "But do not mention d'Urberville to her. Durbeyfield is fine."

"I wish the same, sir," Tess stated with dignity. Just for a fleeting moment at the turning of the drive, between the tall rhododendrons and conifers, he turned his face towards her face. Then, after a moment's thought, he dismissed the notion from his head.

"Well, I'll be damned!" Alec exclaimed when he was alone. "Isn't that funny? Ha ha! What a crumby girl!"

Chapter Six

Tess Arrives at a Decision

Her mother's triumphant reaction on seeing her convinced Tess that something had occurred in her absence. "You've brought them around, Tess," she declared. "What do you mean?" Tess asked.

Her mother replied that she had received a letter. "Mrs. d'Urberville states that she would like you to look after a small fowl-farm that is her hobby. That means she's going to own you as kin."

"But I didn't see her. I saw her son."

"Did he own you?"

"Well, he called me Coz."

"I knew it," Tess's mother exclaimed. "Jacky! He called her Coz. He spoke to his mother and she wants you there."

"But I'm not sure I'll be good at tending fowls," Tess protested.

"Then I don't know who'll be good as you've been brought up in the business," her mother stated. Tess was still reluctant to go and asked to see the letter. It was in third person, informing Mrs. Durbeyfield briefly that her daughter's services would prove useful to the lady to manage her poultry farm. A comfortable room would be provided for Tess if she agreed to come and the wages would be liberal if she was found to be good at her work.

"Oh, that's all!" Tess exclaimed.

"Well, you don't expect her to throw her arms around you to welcome you at once, do you?" her mother asked.

"I'd rather stay here with father and you," Tess replied.

A week later, Tess returned home from the neighbourhood after a failed attempt to gain employment. Her plan was to make enough money in the summer to buy another horse. "The gentleman's been here," one of the children shouted, dancing around the room no sooner than Tess had entered the room. Her mother explained quickly, smiling all over, that Mrs. d'Urberville's son had called on horseback, having ridden towards Marlott

by chance. He wanted to know if Tess was keen on the position offered. For a moment, Tess was rather pleased to know that she was regarded so highly by the stranger, especially when she had sunk so low in her self-esteem herself.

"He's a handsome man!" her mother offered.

"I do not think so," Tess replied coldly.

"Well, you have your chance and I'm sure he wears a beautiful diamond ring."

Abraham confirmed this, saying he had seen the diamond ring.

"I'll think it over," Tess declared, leaving the room.

"She'll be a fool if she doesn't after the conquest she's made," Mrs. Durbeyfield said to her husband.

"As head of the family, I don't like my children going away from home," he replied.

"Let her go, Jacky," his witless wife cajoled him. "Most likely he'll marry her and make a lady out of her. Then she'll be what her forefathers were."

This thought appeared more pleasing to John Durbeyfield. Later, her mother tried to persuade Tess. "What are you going to do?"

"I wish I had seen Mrs. d'Urberville," she said.

"You'll see her soon enough if you settle it."

"I think you should settle it," Tess replied in a restless manner. "I killed the horse and I think I should do something so that you get a new one. But I don't like the fact that Mr. d'Urberville will be there."

The children who were quite taken up with the idea of Tess marrying into wealthy kinsfolk, which they presumed the other family was, began to cry at Tess's reluctance. They also teased and reproached her. Her mother wanted her to go as well. Only her father remained neutral.

"I shall go," Tess was forced to agree, although she insisted that it was only a chance to make money and no other silly thing. But her mother still nurtured the foolish hope in her heart that the gentleman would marry her daughter.

Tess wrote a letter agreeing to the job offer and a reply arrived from Mrs. d'Urberville that a spring-cart would be sent to meet her and her luggage at the top of the vale the day after tomorrow. Tess did think that Mrs. d'Urberville's handwriting was rather masculine though.

"A cart?" her mother murmured her disapproval. "I'd have thought a carriage would have been better for her own kin."

Tess accepted this fate only to procure a horse for her father although, she had hoped to be a teacher at the school. Tess was awake before dawn on the day of her departure. Her mother admonished her when she finished packing and came down for breakfast because Tess was wearing the ordinary clothes of a working-woman. She insisted that Tess had to look her best and washed her hair in a big basin. Then, she dried and brushed it so it looked twice as beautiful. She dressed Tess in her white frock that made her look like a young woman when she was but a child. Tess said goodbye to her father and accompanied her mother and the other children to the base of the hill, at the top of which the vehicle would receive her.

The vehicle appeared as promised and Tess began to ascend the hill alone. They saw Tess approach the spring-cart, on which her box was placed already. But before she reached it, another vehicle shot out from behind the trees, and came to a stop beside Tess, surprising her. This was a more advanced vehicle than

the first one, a spick-and-span gig or dog-cart. The driver was twenty-three or twenty-years-old, smoking a cigar and dressed in dandy clothes and brown driving-gloves. He was the handsome young man who had visited Joan earlier to get her reply about Tess.

"Is that the man who'll make Sissy a lady?" the youngest child enquired. Tess looked undecided as she would have preferred the simple cart. The young man dismounted and urged her to step into his carriage. Tess stared at her family once and that seemed to increase her determination. She ascended the young man's carriage and he mounted beside her, whipping the horse to a canter. The carriage disappeared out of sight quickly. The eyes of all the children filled with tears as this happened. "I wish poor Tess wasn't gone away to be a lady," the youngest one declared. Then, he burst out crying and the action was so infectious that everyone started crying. There were tears in Mrs. Durbeyfield's eyes as well. She sighed in bed that night and her husband asked her what the matter was. "I was thinking that it was perhaps better that Tess hadn't gone," she stated.

"Shouldn't you have thought of that before?" he asked.

"Well, it is a chance for the girl. But if I had the chance again, I wouldn't have let her go till I had found out if the young man is really good-hearted."

"Yes, you should have perhaps done that," Sir John declared.

"Well, if Tess plays her trump card right, as I think she will, he will marry her soon."

"What's her trump card? Her d'Urberville blood?"

"No stupid; her face just like mine!"

Chapter Seven

The End of Innocence

Alec d'Urberville drove speedily with Tess by her side, giving her compliments and leaving the cart carrying her luggage way behind. Tess, who had been rather nervous on vehicles ever since Prince's death, grew increasingly alarmed at Alec d'Urberville's reckless driving and requested him to go slower.

"A brave, bouncing girl like you requests that?" he stated with a smile. They sped in a downward descent now, wheels spinning like a top, with the dog-cart rocking from right to left. Sometimes a wheel was off the ground and sometimes a stone was dispatched over the hedge. Sparks flew from the horse's hoofs to outshine the daylight and the wind pierced Tess's skin, blowing her hair backwards.

She was determined to display no fear, but grabbed at d'Urberville's rein-arm instinctively. "Don't touch my arm!" he warned. "We shall be thrown over if you do so. Grab my waist instead."

She clasped his waist and they reached the bottom.

"Safe! Thank God, despite your tomfoolery." she said angrily.

"Why, Tess, that's temper!"

"It's the truth," Tess retorted.

"Well, you don't have to let go of me so thanklessly the instant we are out of danger."

Tess had not thought about what she had been doing, and sat quietly after gathering her reserve.

"Do it again," d'Urberville urged.

"No!" Tess said firmly. "Please show more sense!"

But d'Urberville would not have no for an answer and tried to kiss Tess. Despite Tess's protests, he kissed her on the cheek. "I have to fetch my hat," Tess said, and got off the cart when he stopped. In the melee, her hat had been blown away. "Where are you going?" d'Urberville asked, as Tess started walking away. "Up again?"

"Never, sir!" Tess said in defiant triumph.

"But it's six miles to Trantridge."

"I don't care if its dozens," Tess replied. He insulted Tess, cursed and swore at her but she would not budge from her decision. Then, d'Urberville tried to drive towards Tess, to hem her between the gig and the hedge. He, soon, stopped as his manoeuvres.

"You should be ashamed of using such wicked words," Tess shouted angrily. "I hate and detest you. I shall return to mother!"

At Tess's temper, d'Urberville's bad temper disappeared, and he laughed heartily. "I like you even more now, Tess. I promise you on my life that I will never do anything against your will."

But Tess still could not be convinced to remount. She walked but did not object to his riding alongside her. Thus, they advanced towards the village of Trantridge slowly. Tess had contemplated returning home but it seemed childish to abandon her resolve, unless she had serious reasons. Besides, how would she face her parents, retrieve her box and risk the rehabilitation of her family on such sentimental grounds? Soon, the poultry farm and the cottage came into view.

The fowls that Tess had to attend to had their primary quarters in an old thatched cottage, enclosed in an area that boasted of having been a garden once. But now, it was reduced to a dilapidated square, with the house being surrounded by ivy. The birds had taken over the lower rooms and the garden where the cottage stood was enclosed by a wall, only be entered through a door. Tess spent an hour the next morning trying to improve her work conditions.

"Mrs. d'Urberville wants the fowls as usual," a maid-servant declared, and realising that Tess did not comprehend, added, "Missus is a blind, old lady!"

"Blind!" Tess exclaimed. She gathered two of the most beautiful Hamburg Chickens in her arms and followed the maid-servant, who also carried two to the nearby mansion. The owner of the estate sat in the drawing-room, a white haired woman who looked about sixty years old.

The maid-servant had placed the fowls on the lady's lap as she had started speaking to Tess and she had examined them from head to tail, right from their beaks to the manes of their cocks.

"Ah, you must be the young woman who has come to look

after my birds?" Mrs. d'Urberville declared, recognizing new footsteps instantly. "I hope you will be kind to them. My bailiff assured me of your capability. Ah, here's Strut! But he isn't lively today, is he? Perhaps he is scared to be handled by a stranger. Phena too! Yes, they are a little scared, aren't you my dears? I think they'll get used to you soon."

She recognized the birds instantly with a single touch and could discern if a single feather was damaged. She also knew what they had eaten and how much; her face reflected criticism that passed in her mind. The birds were returned to the yard and more were brought in to be examined by the old woman. Tess was reminded of a Confirmation, where Mrs. d'Urberville was the Bishop, the fowls the young people presented and herself and the maid-servant, the parson and curate of the parish, presenting them.

"Can you whistle?" she asked Tess after the examination ended.

"Whistle, maám?"

"Yes, whistle tunes."

Tess admitted she could whistle and was urged to practice daily.

"I had a lad who could whistle very well," the lady explained. "But he has left and I want you to whistle at my bullfinches. Since I cannot see them, I'd like to hear them and we teach them airs that way. Show her the cages Elizabeth," she instructed the maid-servant. "You must begin tomorrow as they have been neglected for many days."

"Mr. d'Urberville whistled to them this morning, maám," Elizabeth informed.

"He! Pooh!"

Tess saw furrows of disgust on the old lady's face and then Tess was dismissed. She was unaware that the old lady hadn't heard a word about the so-called kinship. Tess realised that there was no great love between mother and son. But she was mistaken there! Mrs. d'Urberville was not the first mother who was forced to love her son, as well as resent him making her bitterly fond of him.

The next morning, Tess tried practicing whistling. But she discovered that she had lost her former artistic ability. Suddenly, a voice disturbed her concentration. "You look more beautiful than anything in nature or art, Cousin Tess," Alec d'Urberville declared, and the word 'Cousin'

had a mockery in the way it was uttered. "But why can't that pretty red mouth not produce a note? Why! You are rather angry because you can't do it!"

"I might be angry, but I didn't swear."

"Those bullies! My mother wants to further your musical education and that's very selfish on her part. As if looking after those hens and cocks wasn't enough! I'd refuse if I was in your place."

Alec offered to give her lessons and Tess refused. Alec said he wouldn't touch her; and would stand on the other side of the wire-netting and teach her. Tess agreed, and soon, she was whistling under his guidance. Tess was so thrilled at her success that she even smiled at him.

"I'm rather out of mother's good books now," Alec declared. "But if you handle her live-stock well, nothing would please her more. If you want help there, come to me!"

Thanks to Alec's help, Tess found it easy to whistle to the bullfinches and overcame her initial shyness with regard to him. The bullfinches slept in the same room as Mrs. d'Urberville, and one day when Tess was at the window where the cages were, she saw a pair of boots below the

fringe of the curtains, after hearing a rustling sound. Someone was eavesdropping and must have known that Tess was aware of his presence. Tess searched the curtains daily after that but never found anyone within them.

The villagers of Trantridge thought saving money was useless and liked to drink hard. Every Saturday night after work was finished, they liked to travel to a market-town called Chaseborough, about three miles away. They returned in the wee hours of the morning and slept the entire day on Sunday to recuperate from the effects of the alcohol consumption. Tess did not join these excursions for a long time but after pressure from her peers, she consented and actually enjoyed them. But one day, a rather unfortunate incident happened. Tess attended a dance that was rather immoral for her standards. She was attacked by a dark woman called Car Darch, nicknamed Queen of Spades, till recently d'Urberville's favourite. Car Darch had an altercation with Tess. The jealous Queen of Spades was joined by the Queen of Diamonds, a nickname for her sister Nancy and their other friends, to outnumber Tess. Tess was rescued from the catfight by Alec d'Urberville. As his horse sped away with Tess behind Alec, the women who had attacked Tess started laughing.

"From the frying-pan into the fire," one of them declared.

Alec d'Urberville treacherously led Tess into the woods. Tess told him she didn't love him when d'Urberville made advances towards her again. As darkness descended suddenly he left Tess to discover their whereabouts from the top of the slope. When he returned, Tess was fast asleep. That night, Tess would be the victim of a nobleman, just as peasant girls had been for centuries. As Tess's own people would have added, 'It was, to be.' It was, indeed, a piteous situation!

Chapter Eight

The Death of Sorrow

Tess left Trantridge four months after she had arrived there, a few weeks after that nocturnal incident. It was just after dawn when Tess reached the barrier of the vale that needed to be climbed over to reach her birthplace. She saw a man approach her on horseback.

"Why did you leave like that?" d'Urberville demanded. He, then, urged her to return. When Tess told him she wouldn't return, he offered to drive her home. As they neared the village of Marlott, Tess started crying.

Alec d'Urberville apologized for hurting her and offered to pay Tess money so she wouldn't have to work again.

"I refuse to take anything from you and be your creature," she replied scornfully.

"One would think you are a princess, apart from being an original d'Urberville," he laughed. "Well, I know I am a bad fellow! I was born bad, lived bad and shall probably, die bad. But I promise I won't be bad towards you again Tess. Whenever you want to return, all you have to do is write to me. I can't stand the old woman I shall not be in Trantridge as I am going to London for a while but know that all letters will be forwarded."

Tess did not want him to drive her home, and they stopped under a clump of trees. Alec d'Urberville kissed her goodbye and was gone. There was not a human soul in sight but as Tess walked home, she heard footsteps behind her. The man walked so fast that he had caught up with her and wished her good morning before she was aware of his presence. He appeared to be an artisan, and offered to take her basket. She agreed, and they walked together.

"I work for the glory of man all week and for the glory of God on Sunday," the man revealed and proceeded to paint a middle board of a stile on a road leading to a pasture. He wrote words from the Bible on it and they seemed to declare themselves loudly, making the atmosphere ring.

"Do you believe in what you paint?" Tess asked him, as they resumed walking.

"Do I believe in my own existence?"

"What if you were not responsible for your sins?"

"I cannot answer that burning query. This summer, I have walked hundreds of miles to paint these texts on every wall, gate and stile. I leave their understanding to the people who read them."

"I think they are horrible!"

"That is what they are meant to be," the man replied and asked her to wait while he painted another one. But Tess refused and trudged on after taking her basket.

"If you need explanation for these," the man shouted after her, "there's a good man called Mr. Clare of Emminster, who will preach a charity sermon in the parish you are going to."

"I don't believe God said such things," Tess said to herself, as she resumed walking.

Tess was greeted by her surprised mother when she reached home who kissed her in joy.

"My dear Tess, how are you? Have you returned home to get married?"

"No, mother."

"For a holiday?"

"Yes, for a long holiday."

"Isn't your cousin going to do the grand thing?"

"He's not my cousin and he's not going to marry me."

Tess's mother took her inside where Tess told her everything.

"And yet, you won't get him to marry you," Joan exclaimed. "Any other woman would have done it."

"Any other woman, except me."

Tess's mother expressed her disappointment at these events, stating that Tess should have been more careful if she hadn't wanted to marry him.

"O mother! How was I supposed to know?" a wounded Tess exclaimed. "I was a child when I left this house four months ago. Why didn't you warm me that men were dangerous? I never read novels that tell you that sort of thing and you never told me. You didn't help me at all!"

"I thought you would lose your chance if I did so. Well, we must make the best of it," her mother said, wiping her eyes with her apron.

The news of Tess's return spread through the neighbourhood, and many young girls arrived to pay her a visit in the afternoon. These were friends and acquaintances of Tess who arrived in their best clothes to visit someone whom they assumed had made an elevated conquest in life. The rumor went around that the nobleman d'Urberville had fallen in love with Tess. Tess's mother was happy as such a reputation might yet result in finding a suitable match for her daughter. Tess's spirits were also revived with the arrival of the young visitors, who were asked to stay behind for tea. But the next day, Tess awoke to the same sadness that had pervaded her heart. She recovered after a few weeks to attend Church.

As time went by, Tess gave birth to a baby. Tess lived in seclusion for a long time before deciding to take up outdoor work in her village. At lunch time she called up her sister and took the baby from her. Tess suckled the child as the men looked the other way. After the child had drunk its fill, Tess started displaying conflicting emotions; handling the child with dislike one moment and showering him with kisses later.

"She loves the child, although she pretends to hate it, saying she wishes the two of them were in the churchyard," one of the women observed.

"It's a thousand pities it happened to her but it's always the best looking ones as the plain ones are as safe as churches."

Despite her best efforts, Sorrow did not survive. Being the parent of a nameless child was difficult and Tess led a tough life. No wonder the child had been named Sorrow. Tess remained calm at the time of her son's death. Her son had been denied the christening of her child and she know she had done it herself. She now approached the Vicar so that her dead child received a Christian burial. The Vicar refused but Tess was adamant and the Vicar relented so that Sorrow had a Christian burial after all. He was carried in a small box to the churchyard at night, wrapped in an old shawl and buried by lantern-light at the cost of a shilling and a pint of beer to the sexton.

After Sorrow's death, Tess was transformed slowly from a simple girl to a complex woman. She was so aloof that people had forgotten about her crisis. But Tess knew that she had to leave Marlott to escape her past. The opportunity arrived after a long wait, when she received news from a friend of her mother that a skillful milkmaid was required many miles away southward. This opening was for the summer months in a dairy called Talbothays.

Chapter Nine

Meeting the Stranger Again

Tess arrived at the dairy at half-past four, when it was time for the cows to be milked. Tess followed as the cows were led into the yard, and watched as they were milked. Each dairy-girl sat on her three-legged stool, face sideways and right cheek resting against the cow. Tess approached the master dairyman, a strong middle-aged man. He was a master milker and butter-maker for six days and a family man at Church on Sundays. He was fine enough to have inspired a rhyme-

'Dairyman Dick
All the week
On Sundays, Mister Richard Crick.'

Mr. Crick was glad to get a new hand in Tess, as these were

busy days. As the milk squirted from her fists to the pail, Tess was happy that she had secured a future.

It was a large dairy, with almost a hundred milkers under Crick's supervision. Tess's co-workers were friendly but Tess was surprised that one of the milkers was addressed respectfully by all of them, including Mr. Crick. She couldn't see his face, as he was under the cow. But it was obvious that he was not an expert.

"Gently, sir," Crick said to him. "It is knack, not strength that does it!"

"So I see," the man replied, standing up. "I think I have finished although she made my fingers ache."

Tess realized with a start that it was the same stranger whom she had seen at the club-dance at Marlott. She thought he might be an eccentric landowner or a gentlemanly ploughman as he was an amateur at dairy-work.

After the milking was over for the evening, they went indoors and found Mrs. Crick there. She was too respectable to be milking and wore a gown in this hot weather just because the dairy-maids wore prints. Only three maids slept in the dairy-house except Tess, as most

left for their homes. After supper, Tess retired to the large room over the milk-house that was almost thirty feet long. Tess was so tired that she fell asleep immediately but was woken up by the whispered gossip of the two young girls in the darkness.

"Mr. Angel Clare is learning milking. He plays the harp, but never speaks much to us. He is a parson's son and too busy in his own thoughts to notice girls. He is the dairyman's student now, learning farming in all its stages. I've heard he's mastering dairy-work after learning sheep-farming. He's quite a gentleman, the son of the Reverend Mr. Clare at Emminster, miles away."

"An earnest clergyman, isn't he?"

"Yes, the most earnest man in Wessex, and the last of the Old Church sort. All his sons are parsons except Mr. Angel Clare."

Angel Clare had a mouth that was too small and delicate for a man, but something in his manner characterized him as someone who had no particular ambition about his material future. He was the youngest son of his poor parson father, and had come to Talbothays Dairy as a pupil for six months, after making a round

of other farms with the objective of learning the many processes of farming. He had his eyes set on the Colonies or a house-farm in the future. His entry into the ranks of agriculturalists and breeders was not anticipated by anyone, including himself. Angel's father had remarried rather late in life and his second wife had given birth to three sons. Angel was the only son who had not taken a University degree, despite displaying the most promise in his youth.

Three years before Tess had first seen Angel at the dance, his father had received a parcel that was intended for him. It contained a book on philosophy and it appeared sacrilege to the Vicar that his son should be reading such works. He banned his son from taking the Orders, as it shocked him that his own flesh and blood could be against the Church. According to him, there was no point sending Angel to Cambridge either if he did not join the Church.

"What use is a University education if it cannot be used for the honour and glory of God?" the Vicar stated.

"It might be used for the honour and glory of man," Angel reasoned. If he had insisted, Angel might have been sent

to Cambridge. But as his father was against the idea, he gave up the thought too.

Angel spent many years in study and meditation instead, despising distinctions of rank and wealth that dominated English society. He had chosen to learn farming as he was growing older and had to do something. Farming was interesting as it offered a life in the Colonies where intellectual liberty would be on offer. So, at twenty six, Angel was present at Talbothays when Tess arrived there. He had plenty of privacy in his residential quarters and a huge attic running throughout the dairy house, reached only by a ladder. Initially, he spent most of his time there reading and playing the harp he had purchased at a sale. But soon, he studied human behavior by having his meals in the general dining-kitchen with everyone. To his surprise, the companionship was delightful.

Angel barely noticed Tess for many days, being engrossed in a book. Tess spoke little but one day when she did, her fluty voice sparked interest and he looked at her.

"I don't know about ghosts," she was saying, "but I know that our souls can go outside our bodies while we

are still alive."

"Is it so, maidy?" the dairyman asked seriously.

"An easy way to feel them go is to lie on the grass at night and stare at a big, bright star. Fix your mind upon it and you will find you are hundreds of miles away from your body, which you don't seem to want at all."

Angel kept observing her and Tess, conscious of being watched by him, began to trace imaginary patterns on the tablecloth.

"What a fresh and virginal daughter of Nature that milkmaid is," Angel thought and suddenly realised that he had seen her somewhere before, although he couldn't place exactly where.

The cows were milked without choice but certain cows showed a liking for a particular pair of hands. Dairyman Crick ensured that the cows were constantly interchanged so that he wouldn't be placed in a tough spot if anybody left the job. Tess soon, discovered, which of the cows liked her and there were eight among the ninety-five cows who could be milked easily by Tess.

Tess had heard the noises made by Angel in the attic above and was fascinated. One day, she watched Angel

play in the garden, and watched from behind the hedge. Frankly, both the instrument and playing were poor but Tess was still charmed; and had knowledge of neither time, nor space. Tired of playing, Angel walked behind her and saw her. Tess started to withdraw.

"What makes you go, Tess? Are you afraid?" he asked.

"No sir, not of outdoor things."

"So you have indoor fears then?"

"Yes sir."

"What of? The milk turning sour?"

"No!"

"Life in general?"

"Yes."

"Ah, so have I. The whole business of being alive is rather serious, no?"

"It is, now that you put it that way."

"But how does a young girl like you see it that way?"

Tess was silent and he urged her to speak in confidence.

"The trees have inquisitive eyes, don't they sir? The river asks them why they trouble her with their looks and you seem to see numbers of tomorrows in a line, the first biggest and clearest, the others getting smaller. But all of

them seem fearsome as if saying, 'I'm coming! Beware of me!'...But you, sir, can raise dreams with your music and drive such horrible fancies away!"

Angel was surprised that this young milkmaid could have so much depth in her and express such sad emotions. Similarly, it was incomprehensible for Tess why someone like Angel, hailing from a good family should consider it a pain to be alive. It could not be because he was out of his class by milking cows, as he did so with an aim to be rich someday. They were both genuinely puzzled by each other and each hour, each day, brought them closer. Tess wondered if she should reveal her family's association with the famous d'Urberville family but learnt from the dairyman that Angel despised old families. She decided against telling him the same. Tess was the happiest she had ever been as the two kept meeting each other. They met at twilight before milking was done, and walked together to the cows.

Three of Tess's chamber-companions; Izz Huett, Marian, and Retty Priddle, were madly in love with Angel, and all of them fancied their chances to marry him. He confessed to Mr. Crick that he would rather marry a

dairywoman instead of a lady as he wished to take up farming. Tess decided to avoid Angel after that, so that one of her roommates had a chance with Angel, as all of them fancied that he liked Tess. One day, as the girls were walking to Church, they found that a lane leading to it was flooded with water because of the rain. It was impossible to walk through the water without getting wet. Angel saw their dilemma and offered to carry each girl across. After he had deposited the three girls, he returned for Tess.

"I hope I'm not too heavy," she said as he carried her.

"Oh no! But Marian is such a lump! Are you aware that I have undergone three-quarters of this hard work only for the fourth quarter?"

"They are better women than I."

"Not to me. Oh Tessy!" he exclaimed with passion.

The other girls accepted the fact that Angel liked Tess better than them and although Tess denied this before them, she knew that she was madly in love with Angel herself. But when Izz Huet informed Tess that Angel's family had decided on a lady that he was supposed to marry, Tess's heart sunk. But Tess was both surprised and elated when Angel told her that he loved her!

Chapter Ten

The Confession

Angel, unlike Alec d'Urberville, was a man of conscience and his feelings for Tess were genuine. However, as he was still unsure about his life, he could not afford to be married or even engaged. He decided he needed a break and went home. Angel was welcomed warmly by his family, although all the dairy-girls were saddened by his departure. Angel's brothers noticed that he behaved more like a farmer and he noticed their increasing mental limitations. It was clear that there was an enormous gap in both thinking and lifestyle.

The young lady Mr. and Mrs. Clare wanted Angel to marry was Miss Mercy Chant. Angel knew her well as she was the only daughter of his father's friend and neighbour.

"What kind of wife do you think will be suitable for a farmer?" Angel asked his father as they discussed his future plans. "A truly Christian woman who can take care of you," his father replied. "In fact, Dr. Chant's daughter..."

"But she won't be able to milk cows, churn good butter, make cheeses, rear chickens, sit hens and turkeys, and estimate the value of sheep and calves," Angel reasoned.

"Certainly," Mr. Clare said as he considered this point. "A farmer's wife is most desirable. But I think Mercy has all the qualities."

Angel replied that he had no doubt that Mercy was a good, devout girl. But he had already chosen whom he would marry. "Is she a lady?" his startled mother who had entered the study during this conversation, asked.

"She's a cottager's daughter, but a lady in feeling and nature."

Although Angel's parents did not find this news pleasing, they were happy to know that their son had chosen a girl who attended Church. They said it would be foolhardy for Angel to act in haste but they would meet the girl.

Angel held back the details about Tess as he didn't want to hurt their sentiments. Angel's experience had taught him that there wasn't much of a difference between good women of different classes and evil women belonging to the upper and lower strata of society. Foolish women too, were the same in both classes.

Angel's father decided to accompany him on his own mare for a little while when Angel departed, as his brothers had left for a walking tour. He told Angel about a young upstart named d'Urberville.

"One of the ancient d'Urbervilles of Kingsbere?" Angel enquired.

"Oh no! The original d'Urbervilles vanished eighty years ago. This is a new family in Trantridge, which has taken the name."

He told Angel about this young man who had bad tastes, despite having a blind mother to take care of. When he had corrected the young man as per his duty, the young man had insulted Mr. Clare publicly. Angel was angry but respected his father's practice even more now. He also felt he was closer to his father than his brothers.

Angel met Tess as soon as he returned, and expressed

his wish to be married to her. "Oh, Mr. Clare, I cannot be your wife," Tess lamented.

"But why? Are you engaged to someone else?"

"No, but I do not wish to marry you. I only wish to love you," Tess replied. The fact that she had a child before marriage with Alec d'Urberville weighed heavily on Tess's mind.

"Besides, your parents would not want you to marry a girl like me. They'd want you to marry a lady!"

"Nonsense! I've spoken to them, and that is also why I went home."

"But I can never, ever marry you!"

"Is it too sudden?"

"Yes, I did not expect it," Tess lied. Angel said he would give her more time to think it over. Angel was not perturbed at Tess's refusal, being mature enough to realise that when it came to most women, a no would mean an eventual yes. Little did he know that there was a great deal behind this refusal other than coyness. So Angel persisted with his advances and Tess loved him so much that she couldn't refuse any longer. But although

she told him about her family's association with the d'Urbervilles, she could not gather the courage to tell her what Alec d'Urberville had done to her.

Tess wrote to her mother about Angel wishing to marry her and she wrote back to strictly warn her not to tell Angel anything about the past. So Tess decided to tread on the past which was just like a hot, burning coal. Tess's heart was bursting because she could not reveal her terrible secret to the one she loved. It almost seemed like treachery. Everyone in the dairy was happy at the news of the engagement, including the dairy-girls, although they had lost out on love. Mr. Crick was unhappy he'd lose a good worker in Tess though.

It was decided that they would be wedded on Christmas. On Christmas Eve, a day before the wedding, Angel took Tess to town to spend some private time with her. A man from Trantridge recognized Tess at an inn there but did not speak to her as he did not want to hurt Angel's feelings. But Tess was disturbed at being recognized and requested Angel to postpone the wedding. But she failed, and Tess was married to Angel. The day the couple departed from the dairy, a cock crowed

directly at Angel, which was considered a bad omen.
"I don't like to hear him," Tess complained to her husband, urging him to order the driver to drive on.
"Well! An afternoon crow!" the dairyman exclaimed to his wife. "I haven't heard that all year."
"It must be the change in the weather," his wife stated.
"It can't be what you think! That's impossible!"
The couple halted near the village of Wellbridge to rest for the night where their luggage would arrive later in the night. A package arrived there for Angel along with a letter from Mr. Clare, stating that he was sending over the jewels that Angel's godmother had left behind for his wife. Tess tried on the necklace, bracelets and ear-rings that were brilliant. "How beautiful you are!" her husband marveled. "I have a confession to make, Tess," Angel stated. "I hope you will forgive me for not disclosing it to you earlier as I was afraid of scaring you away from me."

Angel told Tess about a difficult period in his life when he had gone astray, after being denied a position in the Church. He had had an affair with a woman but had never repeated the offence.
"I have a confession to make as well," Tess stated, and

told him all about the incident involving d'Urberville and her dead baby. Angel was silent even though Tess repeatedly begged for forgiveness. "Forgive me, just as I forgave you Angel," she pleaded.

"Oh Tess, does forgiveness apply in your case?" he asked. "You are a different person now!"

Angel broke out in the most terrible laughter, frightening Tess to death. It was like a laugh from hell. "Have mercy!" she begged.

"The woman I have been loving is not you, Tess but another woman in your shape," Angel declared. "I cannot stay in this room right now. I shall take a walk."

Tess followed him outside. Angel walked slowly, and without purpose. He was deep in thought and Tess kept pleading with him. "I was a child when it happened, Angel. I know nothing of men."

"You were more sinned against, than sinning, I agree," he replied.

"Won't you forgive me, Angel?"

"I forgive you, Tess, but forgiveness is not everything."

"Do you love me?"

Angel did not reply to this but said insulting words about

her family that were hurtful to Tess. She took these insults only because she loved him above everything else, unlike him. Tess offered to end her life in the river.

"I do not wish to add murder to my follies," Angel replied and asked her to retire to bed. Tess did so and Angel followed later. But while Tess slept on the bed, he chose to sleep on the couch in the sitting room.

Chapter Eleven

Separation

Angel awoke at dawn. The sky was hellish grey as if related to crime. He made breakfast himself, dismissing the cottager's wife who had arrived. He summoned Tess for breakfast, who arrived with a glimmer of hope that died as soon as she saw his serious face. The couple were ashes of their former fires!

"Say it's not true, Tess," he said.

"It is."

"Is he alive?"

"The baby died."

"The man?"

"He's alive."

Angel looked so distraught that Tess urged him to divorce her.

"I cannot do that, Tess. You do not know the law!"

Tess told him she should have ended her life as she had thought yesterday and Angel pleaded with her not to do any such thing. They had breakfast, but their eyes did not meet. After that, Angel went to the miller's to study his business, which had been the main purpose of halting here. Tess began clearing the table, and soon, the charwoman arrived. Her presence was initially a distraction, and later a relief for Tess. At half-past twelve, she left her assistant in the kitchen and waited in the sitting-room looking for Angel to appear over the bridge. His form was visible at one, a quarter of a mile away. She ran to the kitchen so that the meal could be served by the time he entered.

During the meal, the conversation focused on the methods of bolting and the old-fashioned machinery at the Abbey Mill, where Angel had been. Angel left after an hour, returning only at dusk, when he busied himself with his papers. Tess feared she was intruding and got busy in the kitchen.

"You shouldn't work like this, Tess," he said, arriving after a while. "You are my wife, not my servant."

"I thought I was not respectable, and did not want to marry you because of that," Tess broke down in sobs. "But you urged me!"

Any other man would have been won over by this performance. But Angel Clare was a different man altogether! A hard logical interior lay behind a soft, gentle exterior, like a hard metal vein in soft loam. This had caused him not to accept the Church and this stopped him from accepting Tess as well.

"You are more respectable than half the women in England," he stated. "But it's not a question of respectability but of principle."

They lived like this for two days and Angel was so immersed in thought all the time that he was almost ill. "What is to be done?" he constantly muttered to himself. He told Tess that it would be impossible to live with her as long as the other man was alive as technically he was her husband and not Angel. Tess offered the solution that she would leave him and go home. Angel, who had not thought of this, agreed.

"You must not come to me unless I come to you," Angel stated and although this condition seemed severe, Tess accepted it. He gave Tess a good amount of money and told the coachman where to drive her. When the carriage disappeared, Angel turned away, not knowing that he still loved Tess.

On the turnpike-gate on the highway, she had learnt from the gatekeeper who was a stranger, that a man named John Durbeyfield had his daughter marry a gentleman. Sir John, as he was known now, had treated everyone in the parish. Tess felt so sick that she didn't want to go home after hearing this news and entered her village through a back lane, so that no one would see her.

"Tess!" her mother exclaimed. "We thought you are married now!"

"I am, mother."

"But where's your husband?"

"He's gone away for some time."

"Gone away? When were you married? Tuesday?"

"Yes, mother."

"It's only Saturday today, and he's gone away?"

"Yes."

"What's the meaning of this? Nations seem to seize husbands as you seem to get them!"

Tess laid her face on her mother's bosom and burst out crying.

"You told me not to tell him, mother. But I couldn't lie to him and so, I told him! He went away!"

"You little fool!" her mother exclaimed in agitation.

"I know, mother," Tess sobbed. "But he was so good that I could not deceive him. I would do the same thing if I had to do it again. I could not dare to sin against him."

"But you sinned to marry him then," her mother objected.

"Yes, that is the root of my misery," Tess stated. "But I thought he could get rid of me by law if he had a problem. If only you knew how much I loved him and how I was in two minds as to loving him and being fair to him."

Tess was so affected now that she sank like a leaf into a chair.

"Well, what's done is done," her mother declared. "But I wonder how my children turn out to be simpletons more than the children of others."

Then, Mrs. Durbeyfield started shedding tears herself. "I don't know what your father will say about this, for he's

been talking to almost everyone as to how his family has regained its rightful position thanks to your marriage. Poor silly man! What will he do when he knows that his daughter has made such a mess of things?"

Tess's father's approaching footsteps were heard that instant. Mrs. Durbeyfield said she would break the bad news to him herself and Tess kept out of the way by retreating upstairs, from where she could hear everything. Her father entered, carrying a live hen. He had been reduced to a foot-haggler now, being forced to sell his second horse. The news was broken to him by his wife and he was disappointed, more as to what people would say about him, than the actual incident itself.

"But she can make him keep her if he's married her?" he demanded.

"Yes, but she doesn't want to do that," his wife replied.

"Are you sure he's married her? Or is it like the first..."

Tess could not bear to hear anymore. The thought that she could be doubted by her own and her word unaccepted by her own family, was too much for her to bear. She could not, would not live here for long! She took

half of the fifty pounds Clare had given her, handing the rest over to her mother, stating that it was in return for the humiliation and pain that she had caused them. Then she bid them goodbye. The Durbeyfield household had a good time with Tess's money for some time and Tess's mother declared to her husband that the fissure that had risen between Tess and her husband would be hopefully resolved soon.

WHO
COME TO BRAZIL!
FOR ALL AGRICULTURALISTS

Chapter Twelve

Angel and Izz

Angel reached his father's parsonage after three weeks of his marriage. He arrived as a more practical man than before, although he did wonder if he had treated Tess in a fair manner. One day, Angel saw a placard advertising the advantages offered by the Empire of Brazil for the emigrating agriculturalist. Land was being offered there on good rates and Angel was struck by an idea. Tess could join him in Brazil if he went there and his conventions in a new land would be more practical than here to live with Tess happily.

"Oh Angel, how you surprise us," his mother exclaimed when she saw him. "But where's your wife?"

"She is at her mother's. I've come in a hurry as I've

decided to leave for Brazil."

"Brazil? Surely, all of them are Roman Catholics there!"

"They are? I hadn't thought of that."

Angel's mother told him that they were not displeased with him because he had chosen to marry a dairy-girl. "It was only best that we were not present as it would have embarrassed you since you did not choose to marry her at her home. But I wish I could have seen her before you married her or known more about her. We couldn't even send her a present, not knowing what would please her best. Now, you have not brought your wife with you. What's the matter?"

"I have always wanted to keep her away from this house till she comes with credit to you, mother," Angel explained. "But this idea of Brazil is a recent one and she cannot accompany me on my first journey and must remain at her mother's till I return."

"I shall not see her before you leave?" his mother enquired. Angel replied that they would see her after he returned from Brazil.

"Angel, is something wrong?" she asked. "You are not yourself."

BANK

"I'm not, mother."

"Is it about her? Have you had a quarrel?"

"Not a quarrel, but we've had a difference."

"Angel, does this woman's history require an investigation?"

Mrs. Clare's mother's instinct had rightly put a finger on the problem that was distressing her son. "She is spotless," Angel lied.

"Then, nothing else matters. Anything she lacks will be easily made up under your guidance and companionship," his mother predicted wisely.

After breakfast, Angel went to the bank to withdraw all his money. On the way back he encountered Miss Mercy Chant, who told him that she had heard about his Brazilian plan and thought it to be exciting and promising. Angel decided to visit the Wellbridge farmhouse, where he had spent three days with Tess after their marriage. The business of paying the rent of the rooms and returning the keys took him there. Angel had to wait as the farmer and his wife were in the fields. As he waited, he suddenly had a visitor in Izz Huett.

"Mr. Clare, I thought I'd come and visit you and Mrs. Clare, and see if you were well," she said. Angel learnt that Izz had left the dairy as she found it dismal now. She was staying closer to Wellbridge and Angel offered to drop her home. He told Izz that he was leaving England for a year without Tess.

Angel learnt that ever since he had left the dairy, Marian had started drinking heavily and had been sacked by the dairyman. Retty had gone into a state of depression, and Izz had stopped singing. It was clear to Angel that Izz was madly in love with him. "I'm going to Brazil alone, Izz," he said to her. "I have separated from my wife due to personal reasons and may not live with her again. I might not be able to love you but do you wish to come with me?"

"Yes," Izz stated after some thought.

"Do you know what that means?"

"It means that I shall be living with you only for the time you are there. That's enough for me."

"Do you love me very much, Izz?"

"I do."

"More than Tess?"

Izz shook her head. "No," she whispered. "Not more than Tess. No one could love you more than Tess! Why, she was willing to lay down her very life for you."

Angel was stunned at this revelation! He told Izz to forget their idle talk.

"So much for honesty towards you," Izz said, and burst into tears. Angel calmed her down and apologized for having hurt her.

"I forgive you, sir," Izz said generously.

"Promise me something, Izz. Tell Marian and Retty to be good women and tell them that there are more worthy men than me in this world. Tell them to act wisely and well. Thank you Izzy! You have saved me from an act of foolishness and treachery by speaking honest words about my wife. I admit now that women might be bad but they are not as bad as men in these matters. I can never forget you for this very act. We cannot be lovers but we can surely be friends. God bless you. Goodbye!"

So, they parted as friends, although Izz's heart was shattered.

Chapter Thirteen

Hard Times

Eight months had passed since Angel and Tess had parted ways. Tess had left home to work at a dairy near Port-Bredy, preferring to work rather than live on Angel's allowance. She had spent little of the twenty five pounds that had remained with her. The dairy-work lasted till the milk began to lessen and then Tess found occupation in the harvest work that began. Tess was forced to dig into her allowance money after a bout of inclement weather that made working impossible. Tess's money ran out slowly and one day she received a letter from her mother, stating that they were in dire straits and needed money. As her husband was a man of means, couldn't she send them the twenty pounds that they needed?

Tess received thirty pounds from Angel's bankers soon and she sent twenty pounds to her family. She spent part of the remaining money on winter wear and only a little was left to tide over the rainy season. Tess's pride forbade her to ask Angel for more money. Meanwhile, her husband was lying ill due to fever in the Brazilian clay lands of Curitiba. He had fallen victim to the thunderstorms and other hardships that had plagued every English farmer who had been lured there by the tall promises of the Brazilian Government. Tess was finding it difficult to obtain employment and did not wish to go to Talbothays, where she would surely find employment on compassionate grounds. However, she could not bear their pity or words against her husband.

Marian had learnt from Izz that Tess had separated from her husband. The good natured Marian had immediately written to Tess about an upland farm in the center of the county where she was working now, and which needed hands like Tess. Tess made her way to this farm, reaching Chalk-Newton, where she had breakfast at an inn. Tess was troubled to be the center of attention of

many young men here. "I must do something to keep these men away from me," Tess resolved. As soon as she exited the village, she covered her face partly with a handkerchief as if she was suffering from a toothache. Then, she nipped her eyebrows off mercilessly with her scissors. Now, Tess was insured against excessive lechery. "What an ugly maid!" were the words exchanged when the next group of young men saw her. Tears appeared in Tess's eyes out of pity for her own self. "But I don't care!" she said to herself. "I shall always be ugly now that Angel is not there with me. But although my husband will not love me I shall still love him hating all other men and make them think that I'm repulsive."

Despite bad weather, Tess trudged on without rest to finally reach Flintcomb-Ash on the second evening. From the stubborn soil on display, it was clear that the place demanded the roughest type of labour. Tess was determined to stay there and was reunited with Marian again, although Marian was shocked both at Tess's appearance and the fact that Angel had deserted her. Marian took her to the farmer's wife and Tess was

readily accepted as female farm-labour was scarce and welcome. Tess signed the agreement and found lodging at Flintcomb-Ash. She wrote to her parents, informing them about her new address, without mentioning the hardships of the job. The only fat thing on the soil of the Flintcomb-Ash farm was probably Marian and even she was imported.

Flintcomb-Ash was a village that was neither cared for by its lord nor by its residents. But these factors did not deter Tess from working hard. With a unique combination of patience and courage, Tess survived. Marian and Tess worked hard and endlessly, hour after hour. The rain came in the afternoon and work was an impossibility. But they would not be paid if they didn't work, so they continued working.

One day, Marian informed Tess that Izz would be joining them in the farm. But when Izz arrived, it was so cold that it was absolutely impossible to work. The chill had crept in from the polar region. Other than Tess, Marian and Izz, there were two other women in the camp. They were Amazonian sisters and Tess realized that they were

none other than Dark Carr, the Queen of Spades and her younger sister, the Queen of Diamonds. But they had no recollection of Tess and their midnight altercation at Trantridge. Probably, they did not remember her as they had been under the influence of alcohol when the incident had occurred. They did all kinds of men's work in the farm by choice and looked down upon the other three women.

While the women were in the barn, the farmer arrived and had a good look at Tess. Tess suddenly realised that her employer was none other than the man who had recognized her at the inn where she was with Angel. In fact, she had encountered the same man as she was travelling to the farm and had run away from him when he had tried getting too friendly with her. He waited till he was alone with her, and addressed her, "So you are the one who took my politeness so badly? You thought you had the better of me in the inn with your fancy gentleman. You ran away from me the second time. But now, I've got the better of you," he laughed. Tess did not reply. "You thought I was in love with you, didn't you? Some women are such fools! Nothing like a place

like this to take such silly ideas away from your head. Now, are you going to beg my pardon?"

"You ought to be begging mine," Tess replied calmly.

"As you wish. We'll see who is the master here. You have put up a poor show. The rest of the women have done better than you," he said, pointing at the two Amazons.

"They have practiced it before, unlike me. It doesn't make any difference to you as it is task work and we are only paid for what we do."

"Yes, it does. I want the barn cleaned!"

Tess stated that she would work all afternoon, unlike the others who would leave at two. The farmer left and the professional Amazons left sharp at two. Izz and Marian refused to leave Tess alone and helped her with the work. But they spoke about Angel continuously and how he was wrong to abandon Tess. Tess told them that she would not like to speak about Angel. The two continued their conversation in whispers. Soon, an exhausted Izz Huett broke down. She had walked more than a dozen miles last evening to reach here, had slept at midnight and woken up at five. Marian, thanks to her stout figure and

alcohol consumption, took the strain. Tess told Izz to go and rest, and she gratefully disappeared. Marian revealed to Tess that Angel had wanted to take Izz to Brazil with him and had changed his mind only at the last minute. Tess burst out in tears at this disclosure. She tried writing a letter to Angel but gave up as she was really hurt by his behavior. Why hadn't Angel written to her? Tess made up her mind to go and look for her husband. When the weather cleared, she set off, after letting Izz and Marian know of her plan. Exactly a year had passed since Angel and Tess had been married. At noon, Tess was by a gate that led to Emminster and its Vicarage. Tess took off her heavy walking boots to put on her thin and pretty leather boots. She entered the Vicarage but it was empty. It struck her suddenly that it was Sunday and everyone had gone to Church! Tess walked towards the church where the vicar's family was. The churchgoers were walking out, and she immediately identified her husband's brothers, having seen them once before and because they spoke in the same manner as her husband. "That's Mercy Chant," they said of a lady walking ahead of them and Tess stared

at the woman who had been chosen to be Angel's wife by his parents. "Ah, poor Angel!" one of the brothers exclaimed. "If only he had chosen that nice girl instead of that dairymaid! I don't know if she has joined him yet but she hadn't when I heard from Angel a few months ago."

"I don't know," the other brother stated. "He never shares anything with me these days. His ill-chosen marriage has caused our estrangement."

The brothers overtook Tess and joined Mercy Chant. Together, the three reached the summit of the hill, to discover Tess's boots there. Miss Chant decided to carry them to give away to some poor person, and they went downhill. Tess continued walking, tears streaming down her face. "There's no way I can go to the Vicarage now," she thought. "Little do they know that I wore those boots to save the pretty ones that he bought for me."

Tess walked aimlessly for a long time, to reach the cottage where she had breakfast. The streets were empty and the old woman told her that everyone had gone to hear the preaching in the barn by an excellent Christian man. Tess reached the barn, and stood at the back of the

crowd to listen to the distinct voice of the preacher. He was more vocal than Angel's father and Tess's interest was kindled when he spoke about his personal spiritual experiences, that formed his views. "I have been the greatest of sinners," he declared. But a certain clergyman, whom he had insulted initially, had brought about his transformation, he said. His parting words had made him what he was now. But Tess was startled as the preacher's voice had an uncanny resemblance with someone she knew. In a state of great suspense, she moved to the front of the barn. The preacher stood upon some sacks of corn, as he addressed the villagers and the afternoon sun shone on him. It was the face of Alec d'Urberville!

Chapter Fourteen

The Convert

Ever since Tess had left Trantridge, she had never seen Alec d'Urberville. So, this encounter was unexpected but caused more of fear than emotional shock, even though he appeared to be a convert repenting his past sins. It was more of a transfiguration than a reform; the once sensuous mouth now devotionally passionate and the lecherous eye now ferocious. Tess was frozen in her tracks and could not move either forward or backwards. But it was not so unnatural, Tess thought. Christian history bore testimony to the fact that the biggest sinners could be the biggest saints!

As soon as she moved, Alec d'Urberville recognized her. The effect on Alec d'Urberville upon sighting Tess

was far more electric than Tess's own reaction on seeing him. The fire in his speech as well as his eloquence was extinguished immediately. His lips trembled and he struggled to deliver the words he wanted to. His eyes rotated wildly everywhere and came back to rest on Tess again. But this paralysis was only momentary, as he was back to normal as Tess walked out of the barn rapidly.

Tess was appalled at this swing of fortunes and she soon heard his footsteps behind her. She reduced her speed, allowing him to overtake her.

"Tess! It is I…Alec d'Urberville," he declared.

"So I see," she replied coldly.

"That's all? Yet that's what I deserve!" he laughed. "I must bear that. I heard you had gone away and no one knew where. Do you know why I followed you?"

"I do, and I wish you hadn't."

"I understand your saying it and you might think of me as a humbug and sneer at me; but the truth is, that I have wronged you grievously and I felt it is my duty to save you from the wrath to come."

"Well, have you saved yourself? Charity begins at home, they say," Tess stated sarcastically.

"I have done nothing! No amount of scorn that you throw on me, Tess, will equal the amount that I have poured on my own self. It is strange how my conversion happened. The parson of Emminster, old Mr. Clare was responsible for it. Have you heard of this good man, Tess?"

"I have," she replied. Alec d'Urberville told Tess how he had insulted the parson when he had tried to mend his ways. But there was magic in the parson's words and when Alec's mother died, he finally saw the light and had started preaching.

"Stop it!" Tess cried. "I do not believe in such sudden things. How can you talk like this with me after all the harm that you've done to me? Men like you take their fill of pleasure on this earth while darkening the world for girls like me. Then, you think you can obtain a place in heaven by getting converted. I do not believe you! I hate this!"

"Why don't you believe me?"

"Because there is a better man than you, who doesn't believe in such things."

"Who is he?"

"I cannot tell you."

He asked Tess about her troubles and she told him about Sorrow, their child whom she had lost. He was struck mute and demanded why she hadn't informed him. Tess was silent and Alec asked her if she would see him again.

"No!" Tess replied. "Don't come near me."

Alec stepped up to a pillar. He told Tess that it was once a Holy Cross. He asked her to touch the stone and swear that she would never tempt him again. A scared Tess did so and he took her leave, saying he would pray for her.

On the way home, Tess met a shepherd. She enquired if the pillar was ever a Holy Cross.

"Not a cross ever!" he informed Tess. "It is a thing of ill-omen, put up in the wild days by the relations of a criminal who was tortured there. They nailed his hand to a post, and hung him later. His bones lie underneath. It was said that he sold his soul to the devil and that he walks sometimes."

One day, Alec d'Urberville arrived at the farm where Tess was working and wished to speak to her about an urgent matter. He wanted to do missionary work in Africa, and asked Tess to accompany him there as his wife.

"This is a marriage licence," he said, drawing a parchment out of his pocket in an embarrassed manner.

"Oh no, sir no," Tess protested.

"You won't? Why is that?" he enquired.

"I do not love you," she replied.

"Maybe that will happen in time, after you forgive me!"

"I love someone else.""

"You do?" he cried. "But is that morally right?"

"No, don't say that," she exclaimed.

"Your love for this man might be a passing phase."

"No!"

"Yes, why not?"

"I have married him. Do not question me further. We are strangers!"

"Strangers? Who is your husband?" he demanded.

"I cannot tell you."

Alec looked crestfallen and put the licence back into his pocket.

"Where is your husband?"

"Far away!"

"What sort of husband is he to stay far away from you?"

"It is because of you. He found out!"

"Ah, that's sad Tess. But the truth is that he has deserted you," he said, and tried to hold Tess's hand, who pulled her hand away, to leave her glove in his hand. She urged him to leave, and he handed her glove back. "God is my judge, Tess. I meant no ill will by taking your hand," he stated.

Farmer Groby rode up to interrupt their conversation, and reprimanded Tess for ignoring her work. Alec d'Urberville got into an argument with him and Tess urged him to leave. Farmer Brody reprimanded Tess again after Alec had left. Tess wrote a letter to Angel that night, assuring him of her undying love but concealing her hardships.

The day of the Candlemas Fair arrived in February; a day that was most important for agriculturists, as new engagements were entered into for the entire year on this day. After an eventful day, Tess had just finished her dinner when Alec d'Urberville paid her a visit.

"Tess! I couldn't help it," he stated desperately. "I had to come and ask you how you are. I cannot forget you how hard I try. Please pray for me, Tess!"

"How can I pray for you when I'm not supposed to think that God would change his plans for me?" Tess asked.

"You think so?"

"Yes, my husband has cured me from thinking otherwise."

"How can you enslave your mind to his?" he demanded. "He must be a petty man to teach you things like that."

"He never forced me to think so. It is I who has done it."

"When I saw that farmer ill-treat you at the farm, I was mad that I had no legal right to protect you," Alec stated and begged Tess to be his wife again. But she refused and he finally left.

But he returned to the farm later, even more determined to woo Tess. He insulted her husband and Tess struck him on the face with her glove so that he bled.

"Now, punish me!" Tess exclaimed.

"No, Tess. But remember one thing," he said, as his voice hardened. "I was your master once, my lady and I shall be your master yet again. If you are any man's wife, I am the man. I shall return for your answer in the afternoon! You don't know me yet as I know you!"

Chapter Fifteen

Evicted

Alec d'Urberville arrived in the afternoon and watched Tess at work. This only made her work harder to avoid him. She even ignored Farmer Groby's generosity to replace her so that she could join her friend. But Alec was promptly by her side as soon as Tess finished work. "Even after my insulting slap?" was all an exhausted Tess could whisper. "I should be foolish to take offence in anything you say or do," he stated, and offered to walk her home. "I can help you, your parents and sisters, by making life comfortable for all of you," he offered.

"Have you seen them recently?" she enquired.

"Yes, but they had no idea where you were. I found you by sheer luck."

"No!" Tess cried after a while. "I don't want to take anything from you."

Alec left after dropping her and Tess wrote a letter to Angel that night, in which she begged him to rescue her from this pitiable state. The appeal in the form of a letter reached the vicarage, falling into the hands of Mr. Clare. He forwarded it immediately to Angel, although Angel's parents were disturbed that he had chosen to marry an agricultural girl and had to be separated from her as well.

Angel had arrived in Brazil more as an act of desperation than anything else. He had mentally aged a dozen years now and the pathos of life attracted him more now instead of its beauty. He regretted his hasty judgment in abandoning Tess now. He recalled how Izz had stated that Tess loved him so much that she would die for him. Meanwhile, Liza-Lu paid Tess a visit to inform her that both their parents were seriously ill and Tess immediately started for home. Once she was home, Tess devoted herself to take care of her family, by forgetting her own troubles.

One day, when Tess was working with their neighbours in the fields, she noticed a stranger in a long smock frock, working in her plot. Tess assumed he was

a helper sent by her father. Neither spoke to the other but he kept coming closer. As Tess threw dead weeds in the fire, he did the same from the other side. As the fire flared up, the face of Alec d'Urberville was revealed. He laughed when he saw the stunned expression on her face.

"A jester might joke that this is Paradise!" he declared. "You are Eve, and I am the old Other One, who has arrived to tempt you in the guise of an inferior animal."

"I do not think of you as Satan," she replied. "But why are you here, digging?"

"I just wanted to see you, Tess and nothing more. I bought the smock frock so I wouldn't be recognized. I came to protest you working in this manner."

He began to persuade Tess now as to how he could help her sick parents, her brothers and sisters. Tess refused. Suddenly, Liza-Lu arrived with bad news. Their father was dead! Yes, the one who was in more danger had survived. Tess's mother had recovered but her father had passed away. Further bad news was in store for Tess and her family. A depopulation was taking place at Marlott and other areas, and the holdings that were not needed by the farmer for his own hands were let out to tenants or pulled down. All the cottages were needed by the

farmer for his own people and it was decided that the Durbeyfield family would also have to leave after their lease ended.

"I should have never returned," Tess said to herself bitterly, on the evening before the day they had to vacate the house. Alec d'Urberville arrived and offered Tess that he would put up her entire family in his cottage. Tess refused, stating that she would rather ask her father-in-law for money. Alec left cursing. The next day, the family journeyed to Kingsbere, where they had rented some rooms. Tess met Izz and Marian on the way, who had left Flintcomb-Ash as life was rather hard there. They informed Tess that Alec d'Urberville had arrived looking for Tess at the farm. They were headed elsewhere and parted from Tess soon. But it seemed that bad news was following the family everywhere. After they reached Kingsbere, they discovered that the rooms they had rented were let out to someone else only because their letter had reached a little late. Alec d'Urberville arrived yet again to make Tess his offer and she refused yet again. Marian and Izz sensed that Tess was in danger and decided to write to Angel Clare, to protect his wife from the enemy that was stalking her. They dispatched the letter to Emminster Vicarage.

Chapter Sixteen

Angel Returns

The vicar and his wife awaited someone at Emminster Vicarage. It was evening, and after a long wait, the visitor finally arrived.

"Oh my boy! Home again at last!" Angel's mother exclaimed as a figure entered from the darkness. "But it is not Angel! It is not my son!" she exclaimed, as the candles shone on the man's face. Even Mr. Clare was shocked to see his son. He had almost been reduced to a skeleton and resembled a ghost.

"I was ill in Brazil," Angel explained. "I'm all right now." His legs gave away suddenly and he sat down so that he would not fall. It was the tiring journey and the excitement of arrival. Angel enquired if any letter had arrived for him. "I received the last one you sent me after

a lot of delay, and completely by chance. I would have come earlier otherwise," he stated.

Only one letter had arrived, which they hadn't sent to him, knowing he was coming home. Angel read the letter in haste, and threw it down.

"Perhaps we shall never be reconciled again," he exclaimed.

"Oh Angel, don't bother too much about a mere child of the soil," his mother stated.

"We are all children of the soil, mother," Angel replied. "But let me tell you that her father is descended from one of the oldest Norman families."

Angel retired to bed and was unwell the next morning. So, he decided to write to Tess's mother in Marlott, announcing his return. He received a short reply from Mrs. Durbeyfield, stating that they were no longer in Marlott, and that her daughter was away presently. She was unsure when Tess would return but would let him know when she did.

Angel guessed that they were all angry with him and thought they were rightful in doing so. He waited for two more days for a second letter and to regain his strength. The former did not arrive, although the latter did. Angel could not ignore Tess's pleas for help anymore and

started packing to go and find her. Then, he received Marian and Izz's letter.

Angel hired a trap from the inn and headed towards the treacherous region of Flintcomb-Ash, from where Tess had written one of her letters. He learnt that Tess had left from here and although her mother stated that she was not at Marlott, he had no option but to go there and find out where Tess was. Angel arrived at Marlott to discover that Tess's house was taken over by new inhabitants, who did not even know her. All Angel learnt was that John Durbeyfield was dead and that his family had left Marlott.

Angel visited the churchyard, where Durbeyfield was buried. He learnt that the headstone had not been paid for because of lack of money. He immediately paid the mason and learnt the name of the village where Mrs. Durbeyfield was residing now. As the village was a small one, Angel had no trouble finding the house. It was an awkward meeting as this was the first time he had met Joan Durbeyfield. After pleading with her, Angel learnt that Tess was at Sandbourne. Angel immediately left for the station that was three miles away. When the last train to Sandbourne left, Angel Clare was on it.

Chapter Seventeen

Murder in Sandbourne

It was eleven at night when Angel found a hotel room in the fashionable watering-place called Sandbourne and telegraphed his father about his arrival. Angel was tired but could not sleep wondering where Tess might be living in this place. He finally retired at twelve and awoke early the next morning. He went to the post office and enquired about the address of Mrs. Clare and Durbeyfield first. Neither was listed and he tried d'Urberville then. The postman told him that there was a d'Urberville at The Herons, a stylish lodging-house.

Angel reached The Herons, and announced himself to the landlady. "Will you kindly tell Mrs. d'Urberville that a relative is eager to see her?" he said, giving

his name. Tess finally appeared in the threshold as Angel waited in the dining room. He held out his hands but they had fallen to his side. How distasteful he must appear to this beautiful woman now! He was a mere yellow skeleton, he thought. "Tess, can you forgive me for going away?" he said huskily. "Can you come to me now?"

"It is too late!" she said in a hard voice.

"Don't you love me, Tess?"

"Too late!" she exclaimed, as he continued to plead. "You must stay away from me now, Angel! I kept writing for you to come and you did not. He kept on saying that I was foolish and that you'd never come. He was kind to all of us after father died. He..."

"I don't understand, Tess."

"He has won me back," Tess declared and as the full meaning of these words dawned on Angel, his heart sank. "He is upstairs, but I hate him now as he lied to me," Tess continued. "He lied to me that you would not come and you have! But go away now, Angel and never return!"

But Angel was frozen. He realized that Tess had left after some time. He found himself in the street after some time, with no idea where he was going.

Mrs. Brooks, the landlady of The Herons, was not an overtly curious woman. But the strange appearance of Angel Clare would have made any woman curious. She tip-toed to the door of the d'Urbervilles and heard a low, moaning sound emerge from within. She looked through the keyhole to see Tess kneeling over a chair and sobbing.
"What's the matter?" a man's voice enquired from the adjoining bedroom.
"You lied to me! My dear husband came home to me and you had said he never would. You persuaded me cruelly by the means of attending to my family's needs. Now, I have lost him forever!" Tess was writhing and Mrs. Brooks could see the pain on her face. Her lips were bleeding from the pressure of her teeth on them.
"He is dying now. My sin will kill him! You have torn me into pieces with your deceit!" she cried. The man said harsher and longer words and Tess jumped to her feet. Mrs. Brooks, thinking that the door was about to be opened, rushed downstairs. But the door was not opened

and later, the landlady saw a dressed Mrs. d'Urberville leaving. Mrs. Brooks assumed her husband was still in the room and started sewing in her room, directly underneath the room of the d'Urbervilles.

Suddenly, her attention was arrested by a small spot on the ceiling. It grew larger slowly and she saw it was red. The scarlet blot in the middle of the ceiling resembled a giant ace of hearts. Mrs. Brooks got up on the table and touched the spot. It was damp and appeared to be a blood stain! She rushed upstairs but being a woman, could not enter. She listened, and heard a steady noise in the silence. Drip! Drip! Drip!

Fetching a workman from the street, she entered the room with him. He went into the bedroom and returned instantly. "My God! The gentleman on the bed is dead! He has been stabbed with a knife!" he declared fearfully. Soon, the news of the murder had spread throughout the town.

Chapter Eighteen

The Temple of the Winds

Angel left his hotel, and received a telegram from his mother stating that his brother Cuthbert had proposed to Mercy Chant and had been accepted. Angel crumpled up the paper and reached the station, only to discover that there were no trains for an hour or more. Angel found it difficult to wait there and decided to walk to the next station catching the train there. On the highway, he saw a human figure running towards him and he slowed down. Only when the figure had reached closer to him, could he discern that it was Tess.

"I followed you from the station," she explained. Tess was shaking and breathless. Angel didn't say a word but led her to a footpath under the fir-trees away from the prying eyes of people.

"I have killed him, Angel," Tess declared with a pitiful smile. "He came between us and ruined us. Now, he can't do it anymore. I never loved him, Angel. I loved only you. Forgive my sin, Angel, now that I have killed him. Say you love me, dear husband!"

"I do love you, Tess," Angel said, hugging her. "But what do you mean by having killed him? Is he really dead?"

Tess told him all that had happened, and Angel's mind was in a state of feverish excitement.

"I will not desert you, my love," he declared. "I will protect you with all that is in my power."

Angel had intended to go to the first station but instinct led him and Tess to walk together further under the firs, which stretched for miles.

"Can you walk, Tessy?" Angel asked.

"Oh yes, I could walk forever with your arm around me," she replied.

After walking for many miles, Angel brought back food and wine from a roadside inn and they had their meal. They spent the night in an abandoned mansion, with only an old woman as the caretaker. She arrived from the nearby hamlet to open the windows at sunrise and shut

them at sunset. The next morning, Angel fetched food from outside again as well a small tin kettle and spirit-lamp. They spent five days in isolation in this mansion as Tess displayed an unwillingness whenever Angel suggested that they move to London or Southampton.

"All is trouble outside; inside its sweet, lovely and content," Tess declared. "But to think, that once the sight of a bird in a cage made me cry!"

One day, as they lay asleep, they were spotted by the old caretaker who entered their room. She was struck by their innocent appearance and left to consult her neighbours about the incident. Tess and Angel awoke, with a sense that something had disturbed them. It was an uneasy feeling and they decided to leave the mansion, and headed northward. They had to cross the ancient city of Melchester to cross the river via the town bridge. They entered the city at midnight and had walked a couple of miles, when they came across a temple of the winds. The place was roofless and full of towers and pillars, with the wind blowing to make strange noises within.

"It is Stonehenge!" Angel declared.

"You mean the heathen temple?" Tess asked.

"Yes. Older than centuries!"

Tess wanted to rest there when Angel wanted to move on. "This place is so grave and lonely, with nothing but the sky above. There is no one else in the world for me but the two of us, and Liza-Lu," Tess declared. "If anything should happen to me, will you watch over Liza-Lu for my sake, Angel?"

"I will."

"Will you please marry her if you lose me, as you will do shortly!"

"I lose everything if I lose you! Besides, she is my sister-in-law."

"That's nothing my love. People marry sister-laws commonly in Marlott. She is so sweet, gentle, and beautiful, Angel. Liza-Lu has the best of me, without having the worst of me. If she was to be yours, I would be happy, and it would be as if death had not divided us. Will we meet again after death, Angel?"

He kissed her to avoid a reply, and she finally fell asleep.

After some time, Angel saw the head of a man approaching them. Then, he heard the shuffle of feet

behind him, and spotted another figure. They were surrounded by trained men who closed in purposefully. Angel jumped up, hands searching for a weapon, loose stone, anything.

"It's no use sir," the man nearest him said. "There are sixteen of us!"

"Please let her finish her sleep!" he requested the men earnestly who did not object to this plea, watching her like the stone pillars.

"What is it, Angel?" Tess asked as she woke up. "Have they come for me?"

"Yes, my dearest!"

"I am happy, Angel, as this happiness was too good to last. I have had enough of it and will not live to be despised by you," Tess declared, and moved forward. Neither of the men had moved.

"I am ready!" she said.

Chapter Nineteen

Death in the Morning

The fine old city of Wintoncester, once the capital of Wessex, basked in the glow of a fine July morning. Two young people with bowed heads were ascending the long road that led out of the city rapidly as if anxious to leave. One of them was Angel Clare and the other was a tall half-girl, half-woman. She was a splitting image of Tess although of a slight built. It was Tess's sister, Liza-Lu. They moved hand-in-hand, but silently.

The clocks in the town struck eight, just as the pair reached the crest of the great West Hill. Both started at the chimes and turned to watch in paralyzed suspense. Their eyes were riveted on a Gothic structure, an old building,

the middle of which witnessed the ascent of an ugly, flat-topped octagonal tower. Viewed from here, it appeared to be that one blot on the city's beauty. Ironically, these two stared at this blot rather than gaze the beauty of the city.

A tall staff was attached upon the cornice of that tower. A few minutes after the hour had been announced, something crawled slowly up the staff and flew in the breeze. It was a black flag! Justice was finally done and the President of the Immortals had finally ended his sport with Tess. The d'Urberville knights and dames slept unknowingly in their tombs. The speechless pair bent down on the ground as if in silent prayer and remained absolutely motionless for a long time, as the flag continued waving silently. As soon as they had gathered their strength, the pair rose, joined hands again and walked on.

About the Author

■ Thomas Hardy

Thomas Hardy was born in Higher Bockhampton, Dorset, England on June 2, 1840, the eldest son of Thomas and Jemima Hardy. His father was a stonemason and builder, and Hardy inherited his love for books from his mother. Hardy grew up experiencing rural life, which features prominently in his novels. When he was 22, Hardy went to London to work as a draftsman and was influenced by the works of authors like Charles Swinburne, Robert Browning and Charles Darwin. Hardy started writing at seventeen and continued when he was an architect by profession. In 1872, he quit architecture to devote himself to full time writing. His prominent novels include Far From the Madding Crowd (1874), The Return of the Native (1878), The Mayor of Casterbridge (1886), and Tess of the d'Urbervilles (1891). In this controversial novel, that caused debate and criticism, Hardy explored themes that challenged the sensibilities of the Victorian readers, ranging from immoral sex, murder, illegitimate children and the unmarried living together.

■ List of Main Characters

Tess (Teresa) Durbeyfield: She's the main character of the novel. Tess is beautiful and men find her appealing and desirable. She is young, innocent and lacks education, but still provides for her family. Tess is innocent enough not to realize that the world is full of evil, lust, vanity and cruelty.

Alec d'Urberville: He is the heir to the d'Urberville fortune. He brings Tess to his house to seduce her. Alec is a playboy who breaks all rules to get women. He ruins Tess who has his child. Finally, he pays for his sins with his life.

Angel Clare: He is the youngest son of Parson Clare of Emminster, who marries Tess. He abandons Tess after the wedding, after learning about her past. Angel spends the next year in Brazil and after returning to England to reclaim Tess, discovers that she is with Alec. After Tess murders Alec, Angel stays by Tess's side till she is arrested. Angel also agrees to take Liza-Lu as his wife as Tess's last request before she goes to the gallows.

John Durbeyfield: He is Tess's father and a haggler or a middleman who buys vegetables and poultry from wholesalers to sell to retailers. John is uneducated, poor and addicted to drink. The idea that he is the descendant of a noble family is also driven into his head and he is obsessed with this false thought.

Joan Durbeyfield: She is Tess' mother who tries her level best to raise her seven children under extremely tough conditions. She sends Tess to "claim kin" with the d'Urbervilles, but fails to warn her daughter about the dangers of the outside world, the desires of men and the meaning of life and love.

■ Questions

Chapter 1

- *Whom did Durbeyfield meet on his way home? What news did this person give him?*
- *What historical details did the parson reveal about Durbeyfield's ancestors? What was the latter's reaction?*

Chapter 2

- *What was the curious legend involving The Vale of Blakemore?*
- *What made Tess angry? How did her anger disaapear?*

Chapter 3

- *Why couldn't Tess bring herself to dance? Why did she leave for home?*
- *Why did Mrs. Durbeyfield insist on going to Rolliver's herself to fetch her husband?*

Chapter 4

- *What was Rolliver's Inn? Why couldn't one legally drink here? How was this problem resolved?*
- *Why did Tess offer to go with the bee hives to the market? Was this a sensible decision? Explain.*

Chapter 5

- *What was Tess's mother's solution to end their poverty? Why didn't Tess like this plan?*
- *Who was Alec d'Urberville? Describe his first meeting with Tess.*

Chapter 6

- *What were the contents of Mrs. d 'Urberville's letter? What was Tess's thoughts on the letter?*
- *Describe what happened after Tess began to ascend the hill to meet the vehicle?*

Chapter 7

- *How did Tess manage to alight from the carriage? Why did she do so?*
- *Describe the meeting between Tess and Mrs. d'Urberville.*

Chapter 8

- *Who was the stranger Tess met as she returned home? What was his occupation?*
- *Who was Sorrow? How did he die?*

Chapter 9

- *Who was Mr. Crick? What was the rhyme that he had inspired and what did it signify?*
- *What was the gossip that Tess overheard in the darkness?*

Chapter 10

- *Who was Miss Mercy Chant?*
- *Why was Tess apprehensive about marrying Angel? Was it the right decision to marry him?*

Chapter 11

- *Why did Angel say that it was impossible to live with Tess? What was the solution offered by Tess?*
- *What news did the gatekeeper give Tess about her father? What was Tess's reaction?*

Chapter 12

- *Where did Angel decide to go to make a living, and why?*
- *Why did Angel ask Izz to accompany him? What made him change his mind?*

Chapter 13

- *How did Tess's money run out? Explain in detail.*
- *How did Marian help Tess gain employment?*

Chapter 14

- *Who was the preacher in the barn? How had he been converted according to him?*
- *Had Alec d'Urberville really been converted from a sinner to a saint? Give your views for or against the thought.*

Chapter 15

- *Why did Tess decide to go home? Was it the right decision?*
- *Why was Tess's family evicted from their house? Explain in detail.*

Chapter 16

- *Describe the conversation between Angel and his parents after he reached home.*
- *How did Angel discover the address of the village where Mrs. Durbeyfield was staying?*

Chapter 17

- *What happened when Angel finally met Tess? Describe in detail.*
- *How did Mrs. Brooks describe that a murder had taken place?*

Chapter 18

- *Where did Angel and Tess find shelter for the night? Where did Angel propose to take Tess and why did she refuse to leave?*
- *What was Tess's last request to Angel? Why was Angel hesitant about this request?*

Chapter 19

- *Who were the two people who were moving out of the city? Why were they in such a hurry to reach the top of the hill?*
- *Do you think it was right on Tess's part to kill Alec d'Urberville? Give your reasons for the same.*